THE CLUE OF THE
SCRATCHED DOOR

'Roy, *that's our car!*'

THE CLUE OF THE SCRATCHED DOOR

by

STEPHEN MOGRIDGE

Illustrated by Douglas Relf

THOMAS NELSON AND SONS LTD
LONDON EDINBURGH PARIS MELBOURNE JOHANNESBURG
TORONTO AND NEW YORK

THOMAS NELSON AND SONS LTD
Parkside Works Edinburgh 9
36 Park Street London W1
117 Latrobe Street Melbourne C1

THOMAS NELSON AND SONS (AFRICA) (Pty) LTD
P.O. Box 9881 Johannesburg

THOMAS NELSON AND SONS (CANADA) LTD
91–93 Wellington Street West   Toronto 1

THOMAS NELSON AND SONS
18 East 41st Street New York 17, N.Y.

SOCIÉTÉ FRANÇAISE D'ÉDITIONS NELSON
97 rue Monge Paris 5

———

CONTENTS

1	The Scratched Door	1
2	A Coloured Cloth	11
3	A Spy ?	20
4	Beech Close	29
5	Startling News	38
6	Bob's Story	47
7	The Alibi	56
8	Weights	65
9	A Discovery	75
10	Escape	82

CHAPTER 1

THE SCRATCHED DOOR

'THE way Dad carried on you'd think I'd bashed the car to bits. It was only a little scratch along the door.'

'But the car was new, Ian. I don't wonder your dad was peeved. I would have been if I was in his shoes.'

'You're car-mad.' Ian Cooper glanced at his friend, Roy Kenton, with a frown of annoyance. 'I might have known I wouldn't get any sympathy from you. But, honestly, I don't see why Dad kicked up such a fuss over a little scratch. He says he'll have to have the door resprayed and he'll expect me to pay out of my pocket money.'

'Quite right too,' Roy retorted with the hearty cheerfulness of one whose pocket money wasn't in danger. 'Perhaps you'll look where you're going next time. How did you scratch the door, anyway ? '

'Just caught it slightly with my pedal.'

'Then you must have been riding too close.'

'Not really. The gap was too narrow, Roy. You see, I was coming in on my bike and Dad had parked the car on the drive. I thought there was room for me to ride between the car and our garden fence, but there wasn't. You can only find out things like that by trying.'

' So your pedal tore a gash along the side of the new Mini ? '

' Not a gash, Roy, just a slight scratch. The car isn't all that new anyway. Dad's had it just over a month and it was bound to get scratched sooner or later.'

' With you about I suppose that would be inevitable.' Roy grinned. ' But the Mini's practically new. Not even run in yet, I suppose ? '

' Nearly. Dad's been knocking up the mileage at the week-ends because he wants the car to be thoroughly run in before we set off for the holidays. We're going camping in France, you know.'

Roy nodded. ' I'd like to go to France—to see motor racing at Le Mans.'

The boys were sitting on their bicycles at the corner of a quiet side street, having paused to finish their conversation in the warm summer sunlight before parting. They were on their way home to lunch, from school, but no-one would have guessed they were in any kind of hurry. Ian was taking his time complaining that he thought his father was unduly sensitive about a small scratch.

Roy began to edge forward. His home lay straight ahead, over the crossroads, on a new housing estate. Ian's home was to the right.

' I still say I sympathise with your dad, Ian. I should be mad if I had a new car and some careless clot like you scratched it.'

' Some people care more about cars than they do about human beings,' Ian said bitterly. ' I tell you there ought to be a law to prevent parents stopping pocket money, and all you do is to take sides against me and dream of Le Mans.'

' Ah, Le Mans ! ' Roy sighed. He was, as Ian had said, mad about cars. Any car would bring a gleam to his eyes, but racing cars were his special delight.

It was not often that his father, a detective sergeant, could take him to watch motor racing. But Roy never missed a televised motor race if he could help it. He would crouch in front of the magic box with his long legs tucked under him and a look of utter absorption on his freckled face. Ian had often seen his friend entranced in this way. At such times Roy's ginger hair seemed to bristle with excitement as cars whizzed round the tricky bends.

Often Roy added his own engine noises to the sound track, completely carried away, and then Ian would smile tolerantly, sure that he himself had grown out of such childish ways. After all, he was a full three months older than Roy !

Ian's interests were cycling, stamps and photography, in that order. But his paramount interest was in detection. He read every detective story and crime book he could lay his hands on. He was as keen on detection as Roy was on car racing, and often envied Roy for having a detective for a father. Roy wasn't a bit interested in detection, and on those occasions when Ian thought he was on the track of something (occasions which occurred frequently) Roy usually poured scorn on Ian's theories.

'Well, I suppose I must be on my way,' Ian said regretfully.

He set his school cap firmly on his dark, tousled hair and looked up and down the main road to make sure it was clear before crossing. As he did so he heard a car approaching from behind. The engine note was familiar: a Mini, surely?

Ian glanced over his shoulder. A mauve Mini was dashing up, just like the one of which his father was so proud. Its amber flasher was signalling a left turn. Ian held his bike steady with locked brakes and waited for the Mini to sweep round in front of him.

'Same colour as yours,' Roy commented. 'There aren't many mauve ones about here—why did your dad choose that colour?'

'He didn't. Mother wanted it, she's fond of mauve.'

The driver changed down and with a quick glance along the other road turned the car left. As it crossed in front of the boys Ian noticed a long, thin scratch on the paintwork of the passenger door.

'Roy, *that's our car*!'

Ian had every reason to sound startled. He had already caught a glimpse of the driver and knew that it was not his father. Nor in any case had he expected to see his father then. Mr Cooper was certain to be still at work. He was employed by a small electronics firm in the town and though he came home to lunch his route did not take him near Ian's.

The driver of the Mini was wearing a check

shirt and brown slacks. Ian had an impression that he was a big bulky man, whereas Mr Cooper was shortish and thin. The man's face was largely hidden by dark sunglasses.

'You mean it's *like* your car, Ian,' Roy corrected, unperturbed. 'The number's different.'

Ian was just quick enough to check the rear number plate as the car sped away.

'It isn't our number, Roy. But the scratch on the door——'

'That's easily explained. The poor chap's probably saddled with a clot of a son like you.'

'Come on.' Ian stood on his pedals. 'If that is our car——'

'No use giving chase,' Roy protested. 'It's a car, and we haven't time.' But he caught up with Ian all the same.

The boys raced along and were able to keep the mauve Mini in sight, for the road was a straight one. Side streets branched off at intervals. The car was still visible in the distance when it braked and turned into one of the side streets on the right.

The boys soon reached the turn and found it was a short cul-de-sac. No Mini was in sight. No car at all.

'This was the turn, Roy?' Ian glanced at his friend for reassurance.

'Yes. I'm certain. It was opposite the telephone box.'

Roy cycled on slowly, looking right and left. The houses on either side were modern, with detached garages. As the gardens were new they were not overgrown and visibility was good. The boys soon spotted the mauve Mini. It had been driven into the garage of a house near the far end of the cul-de-sac and the man in the check shirt was just closing the garage doors.

Ian managed to get another look at the number plate, confirming that it was not the number of his father's car. Then the garage doors were locked and the man sauntered to the front porch of the house, jangling keys from his hand as he walked.

'Another one of your wild-goose chases, Ian,' Roy grumbled. 'That isn't your car, as I told you. The chap obviously lives here.'

'But the scratch!' Ian protested, turning slowly on his bicycle. 'I could have sworn it was the scratch I made with my pedal on our car. It was just like it.'

'If it had been made by a bicycle it would be the same sort of scratch,' Roy pointed out. 'Now let's get home for lunch. We'll be late.'

'Wait.' Ian had noticed a little girl playing in the front garden of one of the houses. She was near the gate and watching them curiously. 'Let's ask that girl if she's seen the Mini before.'

Roy shrugged. 'How suspicious can you get, Ian? You're potty. Just because you saw that scratch you jump to the conclusion that it's your car, but it's a crazy notion, man. Crazy.'

Ian ignored his friend's nattering and approached the little girl with what he hoped was a winning smile. After a few words of greeting he put the question he had been leading up to.

' Have you seen that little mauve car before ? '

' Oh, yes. It's Mr Glover's.'

' Was that Mr Glover driving it just now ? '

' Yes. Mostly Mrs Glover drives, but sometimes he goes out by himself. Why ? '

' I just wondered. My Dad's bought a car like that and I thought the colour was rather unusual.'

' I like the colour, but the car's not new. The Glovers have had it for, oh, almost as long as I can remember.'

' How old are you ? '

' Five next month. How old are you ? '

' Practically grown up.' Ian grinned. ' All the same I shall be in trouble if I'm late for lunch, so I must go now. 'Bye.'

The girl was something of a chatterbox and reluctant to let him go. She said that her name was Louise Martin and offered to show the boys her doll, but they waved and rode off.

Roy nattered all the way back to the corner where they parted. He reminded Ian of previous wild-goose chases undertaken in the spirit of detection, not forgetting an incident known as the Antique Coal-Scuttle Case, which was a sore point for Ian.

' That was the one and only time my father was fool enough to listen to your theories,' Roy reminded him. ' He even went to the shop with you because he thought you really had seen the old dealer take those things, but you were proved wrong.'

' The man who never made mistakes never made anything,' Ian retorted defensively. ' I still think that scratch on the Mini looked like the one I made, and I *should* recognise the scratch. Dad made me look at it long enough.'

' You never allow for coincidences, Ian. Your dad's Mini isn't the only one in England with a scratched door.'

' Maybe not, but it *could* have been stolen. The thought flashed through my mind the moment I saw the scratch. Dad leaves his car in that small park behind his works—anyone could easily take it.'

' If it had been stolen it's hardly likely, is it, that the thief would have driven it home and put it in his own garage in the same town ? He would have driven it miles away, probably to London.'

' I suppose so.'

' Well, see you later, Sherlock Holmes.'

Roy turned away, leaving Ian to ride on, sunk in thought. He *had* felt sure the scratch was the one he had made on his father's car. The model of the car and the colour were the same too, only the number was different. That might have been changed, of course. Car thieves were clever at changing number plates. However, the car had been garaged quite openly and Louise said it had belonged to the Glovers for a long time, so it couldn't have been the mauve Mini belonging to Ian's father.

Ian decided that the affair of the scratched Mini must be one of those coincidences which Roy insisted should be ignored. It was not easy to try to forget the matter, but Ian was helped to think about other things by his mother, who gave him a piece of her mind for arriving late for his lunch.

'You must have been dawdling, Ian dear. I do wish you'd try to come straight home at lunch time—you know you don't have long and you mustn't waste time. You're twenty minutes late and I've had to keep your food hot in the oven for ever so long.'

'Sorry, Mum.'

'You know I like to start you off first. Daddy will be here in a minute. Whatever were you doing?'

'Well, it was like this . . .' Ian crumbled a piece of bread and wondered how best to tell his story. Mrs Cooper was certain to frown upon any attempts at detection. She had been against detection as a career ever since the Antique Coal-Scuttle Case. And Ian knew very well that his father was equally prejudiced. Life was difficult for a would-be detective.

'Well, it's to do with Roy, and it's rather complicated. . . .' Ian hesitated. 'Perhaps I'd better keep the story until this evening.'

'Hoping I might have forgotten to ask by then?' Mrs Cooper laughed and patted Ian's dark head affectionately. 'I know you. Come on, tell me now.'

'Well . . .' Ian saw there was no hope of escaping. 'Well, Roy was talking to me at the corner.'

At that moment the telephone rang in the hall, to Ian's great relief. He hoped it was one of his mother's really talkative friends. Anyway, the call would certainly keep her for a few minutes. She was involved in so many of the town's activities—Civil Defence, Red Cross, Mothers' Union, Townswomen's Guild.

Hoping to escape the need for explanations Ian settled down to his meal, but a cry from his mother startled him.

' Ian, it's Daddy—he can't get home to lunch. The car's been stolen.'

CHAPTER 2

A COLOURED CLOTH

IAN leapt up from the table. 'Then it *was* our car !
I saw it, Mum. I know where it is.'

He rushed out into the hall, but was too late to
catch his father on the line. Mrs Cooper had just
replaced the telephone receiver.

'Now what are you gabbling about, Ian ? ' she
asked, with the resigned tolerance of one used to
his excited interruptions. 'Isn't it enough for
me to be told our car's been stolen without you
making all this song and dance ? Do get on with
your dinner or you'll be late for school.'

'But Mum, I saw our car just now. I know I
did.'

Mrs Cooper studied him thoughtfully. 'Are
you *sure*, Ian ? '

'Certain. I recognised the scratch on the door.
I followed the car with Roy—that's what made
me late.'

'So you were playing detective again ? '

There was something about the way his mother
spoke that made Ian realise he was going to have a
difficult time convincing her.

'I *did* see our car, Mum,' Ian told her earnestly.
'I followed it with Roy.'

'On your bicycles ? ' Mrs Cooper raised her
eyebrows.

'We kept it in sight, and saw it turn into a side road.'

'Did you see the number of the car?'

'Yes—it wasn't our number, but of course the thief would have changed that already. We gave chase just as fast as we could—simply tearing along like mobile police on motorcycles—and we were in time to see the car being shut up in the garage of a house.'

'What was the name of the road?' Mrs Cooper glanced at the telephone. 'If you really think it was our car we could ring the police station. Daddy's on his way there now.'

'I'm sure it was our car, Mum, as I've told you. The road was a cul-de-sac. Beech Close. I spoke to a little girl there and she told me the name of the man who was driving our car—Mr Glover. I expect he's going to spray the car a different colour now, then he'll sell it and——'

'Glover? Beech Close?' Mrs Cooper was not impressed. In fact she merely sighed and, leaving the telephone, propelled Ian before her to the dining-room. 'Sit down and get on with your dinner. You've wasted quite enough time as it is. You and your detective larks.'

'But Mum, we must tell the police.'

'Nothing doing, my lad. No more wild-goose chases like that last one we had, with all that embarrassment.'

'But this isn't a wild-goose chase, Mum. You were nearly going to phone the police just now. What made you change your mind?'

'Because I happen to know Mr and Mrs Glover

of Beech Close. Mrs Glover is a member of the Townswomen's Guild and our Dramatic Society.'

' But——'

' *And*,' Mrs Cooper continued in a louder voice, pointing to Ian's plate to remind him to get on with his lunch, ' *and* the Glovers have a mauve Mini, my lad. In fact, it was because I liked the colour of their Mini that I made Daddy buy one the same. Now, Ian, I don't want to hear any more of your wild theories.'

' But the scratched door, Mum ! It must have been our car.'

' Don't tell me you could recognise a car by a little scratch like that.'

' It wasn't a little scratch. You know how Dad carried on about it.'

' That's because he always fusses over anything new. He didn't mean all he said, as you should know by now.' Mrs Cooper ruffled Ian's hair and went to fetch his sweet from the kitchen. ' As a matter of fact I hardly noticed the scratch. It didn't take the paint off right down to the metal.'

' Dad said he'd have to get the door resprayed.'

' He only told you that to make you more careful in future. I suppose you were worried about the threat to your pocket money ? ' Mrs Cooper laughed.

' Yes,' Ian admitted. ' 'Specially as I particularly want to buy some stamps next week. There's a new Dutch issue.'

' Well, don't worry. Your father told me he thinks he can polish out the scratch.'

'Good.' Ian was relieved. 'He hasn't tried yet, has he?'

'I don't think he's had time. You only did the damage on Saturday and we went out all Sunday.'

'And Monday and Tuesday Dad was at work,' Ian mused. 'He certainly hadn't done anything by yesterday evening because he was still carrying on at me about the scratch. He won't have polished it this morning, so the scratch must still be there, Mum.'

'Maybe. But if you saw a scratched Mini don't jump to the conclusion that it's ours. There's such a thing as coincidence, you know.'

'But——'

'Not another word,' Mrs Cooper said firmly. 'I don't want to hear any more of your theories, Ian. Just remember the coal-scuttle business.'

Ian watched his mother as she bustled off to the kitchen. He realised that it was hopeless to try to convince her that he had seen his father's car, and even his own certainty was shaken.

Had it really been his father's car? Had that scratch on the door been the one he had made with his pedal? Or was it a scratch rather like the one he'd made? Just coincidence?

When he met Roy after lunch his friend had no hesitation in deciding.

'Of course it wasn't your dad's car, Ian. Look, your mother knows the Glovers, she knows they have a mauve Mini, and the little girl told you the Glovers had a mauve Mini. Also the number wasn't your number.'

'That could have been changed.'

'You're nuts,' Roy retorted rudely. 'Once your suspicion has been aroused you won't listen to reason.'

'It's that scratch——'

'Oh, do shut up about that scratch,' Roy growled. 'You've done nothing but bleat about it since Monday morning. First it was a threat to your pocket money, now it's an important clue to the Case of the Missing Mini. Honestly, Ian! Didn't the coal-scuttle affair teach you not to jump to conclusions?'

'But that *could* have been our Mini, Roy.'

'It could have been Santa Claus in his sleigh. There's another point you haven't considered— why should anyone who already has a mauve Mini go out and steal another one?'

'I can't think. But I do know one thing, Roy. We ought to have a closer look at that Mini in the Glover's garage.'

'*We?* Count me out of any wild schemes of yours, Ian.'

'Suppose we both go along after school. We could offer to wash the car. Say we want to earn a bit of extra pocket money to buy something special, or some yarn like that. Then we could get a good look at the Mini.'

'What for? To admire that scratch and compare it with your masterpiece?'

'If we can manage, Roy, we ought to be able to check on the engine number while we wash the car. That will prove if it's our car, because I don't suppose there's been time to alter the number of the engine yet—it's stamped on the block, you know.'

Roy ran a hand through his ginger hair and stared at his friend with almost open-mouthed amazement. ' You're really serious, Ian ! '

' Of course I am. I'm still thinking about that scratched door.'

' Coincidence, you chump. Come along, or we'll be late for the Haybag's jaw on history.'

The boys joined the stream of others making for the classroom and for a while Ian's mind was forcibly drawn from the mystery of the Mini. Not that he concentrated entirely on his lessons— his thoughts often strayed to the scratched door.

When school was over for the day Ian and Roy cycled to the corner where they had paused on their way home to lunch. Roy was still reluctant to become involved in Ian's ' case '. He stopped at the kerb.

' If you're scared you needn't come,' Ian challenged. ' But I'm determined to have a crack at looking at the engine number of that Mini.'

' I'm not scared,' Roy retorted briskly. ' I just think you're nuts. That car *can't* be your dad's.'

' Well, if we manage to look at the engine number we shall know for certain. It's the only thing we can do, because I don't suppose you can persuade your father to search the Glovers' garage on suspicion ? '

' Certainly not. Dad won't listen to any more of your theories for a long, long time.' Roy looked down the road to the distant telephone box by Beech Close. ' Tell you what, I'll come as far

as the gate, but I'm not going up to the door to
spin any yarns.'

'Coward!' Ian grinned. 'No wonder you're
not very bright at Bob-a-Job week.'

The two boys rode to Beech Close and cycled
slowly down the cul-de-sac. Mr Glover's garage
doors were closed.

'He's out, Ian.'

'Don't sound so relieved, Roy. I'm going to
ring the bell.'

Ian propped his bicycle against the garden fence
and walked up to the front door.

Beech Close was quiet. Some of the residents
were out at work, others were sitting in their
gardens enjoying a summer afternoon treat of tea
on the lawn. While he waited on the Glovers'
step for an answer to his ring Ian noticed Louise
Martin playing on the lawn behind her house.
She seemed to be giving a dolls' tea party.

The Glovers' house remained silent. Ian
wondered if they were taking tea on their lawn.
He decided to walk round the house by way of
the concrete path which separated it from the
garage. This path widened into a little yard by
the back door and Ian was delighted to see that a
side window in the garage looked on to the yard.
He peered through the window and his hopes were
dashed. The garage was empty.

Disappointed, he walked past the back door and
made sure no-one was in the garden. Then he
returned to the garage window and peered in for a
longer survey.

On a shelf under the window he noticed two

tins of car polish and some cleaning cloths. One of the cloths was coloured mauve. It had evidently been used for cleaning the Mini.

There was a door beside the window, the side door to the garage. Ian tried it, expecting to find it locked, and to his surprise it opened. For a moment he hesitated, then he entered.

His first move was to examine the mauve polishing cloth. It was still damp. He guessed it had been used that afternoon. To polish out that scratch on the door ?

Ian looked round the garage. At the end a narrow bench was littered with an assortment of tools and the kind of clutter that accumulates in garages. Old tins, empty jam jars, a box of rusty nails. More clutter was stored under the bench. Paint tins, a watering can, some bundles of firewood, an assortment of flower pots. Along the walls gardening tools hung from nails. A mowing machine stood in one corner, beside the bench.

The garage had a tiled roof, and boards had been laid across the beams so that more clutter could be stored in the apex of the roof, under the rafters. Quite a large platform had been made. On it Ian could see a couple of old trunks and some oil paintings. A pair of folding steps hanging just inside the door was obviously used for access to the roof platform.

Ian was tempted to take them and climb up to investigate. He thought he might find the number plates of his father's car—if it had been stolen by Mr Glover, and the number plates changed. But at any moment the Glovers might return. Ian glanced out of the window. The coast was still clear, so he went back to look under the bench. Among the clutter there he had noticed two cardboard boxes. He found one contained empty jam jars. The other had some oily rags on top, and fir cones below the rags, possibly kept for firelighting. There were certainly no number plates. Nothing that could be considered a clue.

Ian let himself out of the garage and returned to Roy, who had begun to fidget.

'You were hours, Ian. What did you find?'

'The car's gone. But I saw a wet polishing cloth, all mauve polish. I believe Mr Glover's been trying to polish out that scratch and now he's driven the car to London to sell it.'

CHAPTER 3

A SPY ?

Roy was not impressed. He refused to consider Ian's theory seriously.

'You're twisting the facts to fit what you think happened, Ian, and Dad says that's the worst thing you can do as a detective.'

'I'm *not* twisting facts, Roy. That polishing cloth was still damp and the Mini we saw Mr Glover driving at lunch time was clean. It didn't look as if it needed polishing, so why had Mr Glover been working on it ?'

Louise had seen them now and was in her front garden waving. Ian went over to her and asked her when the Mini had left.

'Not long ago.' Louis considered, frowning and cradling her doll in her arms. 'Mr Glover was driving—I expect he was going to meet his wife. I haven't seen her since they both went out in their car after breakfast. I 'spect she's been to London shopping. My mummy goes to London shopping sometimes.'

'You think Mrs Glover went by train ?' Ian asked.

'Yes. Mummy says it's quicker than going by car.'

Ian looked at his watch. If Louise had guessed correctly then Mr Glover had only gone to the station to meet his wife, and the Mini should return at any moment. The fast train from London must have arrived a few minutes ago. The town had a good train service and the journey to London took under an hour. By car it was much longer because of traffic delays.

'Did you see Mr Glover polishing his car this afternoon, Louise ? ' Ian asked.

'No.' Louise was definite. 'He can't have, because the car wasn't outside. If he cleans it he always has it on the drive with the garage doors open.'

'And they were shut all the afternoon ? ' Ian asked.

'Yes.'

Ian tried to catch Roy's eye, but Roy looked away.

'Do you want to see Mr Glover ? ' Louise asked. 'Why have you come here again ? '

'Well, actually we wondered if he'd like his car washed.' Ian told Louise the story he had prepared about wanting to earn some pocket money.

Louise considered and shook her head. 'I'm sure Mr Glover won't help you. He often washes his car, and polishes it. I think he enjoys polishing it, because he hasn't much to do.'

'Doesn't he go to work ? '

'No.'

This time Ian did catch Roy's eye. The suspicious points were increasing.

'Mrs Glover doesn't go to work either,' Louise said. 'She spends her time shopping, I think, and Mummy says she's always in the town having coffee in the morning.   She drives down to the car park practically every day.'

Roy edged away impatiently on his bicycle and called to Ian to come along.   Ian guessed that his friend was thinking about tea, but if the mauve Mini was about to return it would be a good idea to wait and Louise provided the best possible excuse.   So to Roy's evident annoyance, Ian asked Louise about her doll.

This subject interested Louise far more than the comings and goings of the Glovers.   She talked with great animation and told fanciful stories about the things her doll had said and done.

Her vivid imagination rather shook Ian.   He wondered if she had made up any of the things she had told him about the Glovers and the mauve Mini.   A young chatterbox with such a vivid imagination was not exactly a reliable witness, and after ten minutes or so of dolls' talk Ian decided her saying that Mr Glover had gone to the station to meet his wife was nothing more than a wild guess.   The Mini had not returned.

Another point struck Ian.   Would Mr Glover have closed the garage doors and the drive gates if he had only gone down to the station ?   At lunch-time the gates at least must have been open, or the car wouldn't have been in the garage by the time the boys arrived on the scene.

' Louise, when the Glovers go out in their car do they usually shut the garage, or leave it open ? '

Louise looked up sharply at Ian, jerked out of the long story she was telling about her doll and a teddy bear.

'You're not listening,' she accused.

'Oh, yes I am. But I just remembered the garage doors are shut now, and the gates. If Mr Glover's only gone to the station——'

Louise interrupted. 'Perhaps he hasn't gone to the station. The doors are usually open. Mrs Glover always leaves them open in the morning when she goes shopping, and the gates. She only shuts them if she's going to be out in the car all day.'

'Were the doors open this morning?' Roy asked, startling Ian by this sudden show of interest.

Louise nodded. 'They're often open in the daytime anyway, even when the car is in the garage.'

Roy mounted his bicycle again. 'Well, as they're closed now it means that Mr Glover must have gone out for a long time. Perhaps he's driven up to London to meet his wife. Come along, Ian, or we'll miss our teas.'

Ian managed to tear himself away from the talkative Louise. As they rode home he explained to Roy that he had only gone on talking to Louise because he wanted to wait for the return of the Mini.

'And we did find out a few more things from her chatter, Roy.'

'All of them suspicious—in your eyes, of course.'

'Well, aren't they suspicious?' Ian challenged. 'Don't you find it strange that Mr Glover should have polished the Mini behind closed doors this afternoon, when it's a lovely summer afternoon and he usually cleans the car on the drive ? '

' Perhaps he wanted to be in the shade.'

' He would have been in the shade from the house if he'd had the car on the drive this afternoon.'

' Yes, I suppose he would. Perhaps he didn't want Louise to stroll along and chatter to him. I've no doubt she does do that sort of thing.'

' I don't think her mother allows her outside the garden, Roy. Another thing—Louise says Mr Glover doesn't do any work.'

' Quite a lot of people don't do any work, but that doesn't make them crooks. He may have won a football pool or something.'

' Now you're twisting facts to fit your theories, Roy. You think I'm crackers to suspect the Glovers of taking our car and you're determined not to believe that anything is suspicious.'

' No. It isn't that, Ian. I'm sure you're barking up the wrong tree. What earthly reason can the Glovers have for taking your car, when they've got a Mini just like it ? '

' If we could work that puzzle out it might help a lot.' Ian frowned. ' You know, Roy, it could be that they took our Mini *because* it's exactly like theirs.'

' But why ? '

' Why do crooks steal cars ? '

' Either to sell them, or else to use as getaway cars for a bank robbery or a wages snatch.'

' A getaway car . . .' Ian mused. ' Could be the Glovers are planning a bank robbery.'

'Don't be daft, Ian. If they were they'd
pinch a really fast car for the getaway, not an
ordinary Mini. Yours isn't a hotted up model, is
it ?'

'No. But perhaps the Glovers' Mini is a
special job and they're planning to confuse the
trail somehow by changing the cars over.'

The boys had reached the corner where they
usually parted and they stopped to talk. Ian tried
to work out a theory about swapping cars, but
only got involved in complications that didn't
make sense.

He had to admit that he couldn't see how
juggling with two mauve Minis would help the
Glovers to carry out a bank robbery.

'That leaves us with the other possibility, Roy.
The Mini's been stolen to sell on the crooks'
market.'

'Could be.' Roy nodded.

'I bet I'm right about that polishing cloth, Roy.
Mr Glover's been working on the scratch and now
he's taken the car to London to sell.'

'I still don't see why he should have stolen your
Mini when he had one like it,' Roy objected.
'You'd think he would have taken something else.
A bigger car.'

'No. Our Mini was safe and easy, Roy. He
could drive it home and put it in his garage without
attracting any attention. The neighbours wouldn't
realise it was a stolen car, because they'd think it
was his.'

'Hm.   That makes sense,' Roy admitted
cautiously.

'Tell your father what we've discovered, Roy,' Ian urged. 'We must get cracking. Your father ought to arrest the Glovers at once.'

'On what evidence?' Roy laughed. 'I'm not breathing a word of this " case " of yours to Dad. Remember what happened last time.'

'But if I'm right and you tell your father, Roy, we'll be helping him to get promotion.'

'If it's anything like your coal-scuttle case we'll be helping Dad to get the sack.'

'Oh, don't keep bringing that up, Roy. This is a completely different case.'

'Yes, but you haven't *really* got anything to go on except suspicions. And Dad won't take any notice of them, I'm sure. Anyway, your Mini may have been found by now for all we know. It may have been abandoned somewhere this afternoon while we were in school.'

'Of course not, Roy. Mr Glover has it. Do talk to your father about what we've discovered.'

'Tell you what, Ian. I'll find out from Dad, if I can, what he knows about the theft of your Mini. I'll come round to you after tea.'

'Wouldn't it be better if I came round to you? Your father might be home by then.'

'Just what I was thinking.' Roy grinned. 'That's why I thought it better to come round to you. Dad doesn't like to be pestered.'

Ian grimaced and the boys parted. As he rode home Ian thought over the puzzling aspects of his new ' case '. He felt certain he was on the track of the stolen Mini and his certainty increased when his mother told him there had not been any news

of the car. The police had certainly not phoned
to say it had been found.

Mr Cooper had to take a bus home from
work and he was not in the best of tempers when
he sat down to a late tea. Nor did his mood
improve when Ian's suspicions of the Glovers
were told with urgency and a plea for instant
action.

' You know what you are for making mountains
out of molehills, Ian,' Mr Cooper said grumpily,
stirring his tea. ' You've built up all this mountain
of suspicion from one simple little thing—a
scratched door. As for your wild theories, they
don't make sense.'

' But everything adds up, Dad,' Ian insisted,
unabashed. ' The Glovers knew we had a mauve
Mini. Mum's talked about it to Mrs Glover.
And they knew where you parked it while you
were at work. They must have realised it would
be easy to steal.'

' I'll grant you have a point or two there, Ian,
supposing the Glovers are crooks. But I can't
see why they should want a second mauve Mini.
Oh, I know your theory about it being easy to
steal and hide in their garage, but I'm not con-
vinced. If they wanted to steal a car to sell, I
think they'd have taken a bigger one, worth more
money.'

' But ours is practically new, Dad,' Ian pointed
out. ' Anyway, they may have taken it to use for
a robbery and not to sell.'

Mr Cooper gave a short, disbelieving laugh.
' Frankly, Ian, I think that theory is absurd. If

the Glovers are planning to rob a bank they won't use a car exactly like their own to do the job with.'

' No . . .' Ian shrugged. ' Then they must have stolen our Mini to sell.'

' Nonsense,' Mrs Cooper said briskly, handing Ian some more bread and butter. ' I'm sure the Glovers aren't crooks. You've too much imagination, Ian.'

' How well do you know them, Mum ? '

' I've only met him once or twice, but I often run across Mrs Glover. She's a very sociable woman. Oh, she can't be a crook, Ian.'

' Have you had her here to tea, Mum ? Have I met her ? '

' No, she hasn't been here. I meet her at our women's gatherings, and I sometimes see her in town having morning coffee in that café by the roundabout. She takes such an interest in everything. I'm sure crooks aren't nice sociable people.'

' Perhaps Mrs Glover has a reason for being sociable, Mum,' Ian suggested darkly. ' Perhaps she's acting as spy for a gang of payroll snatchers and bank robbers, and now they're all set to carry out a raid using our Mini.'

CHAPTER 4

BEECH CLOSE

IAN begged for instant action, urging his father to go to the police. But Mr Cooper stubbornly refused to get excited and his wife insisted that Mrs Glover was much too nice to be a crook.

'Do forget about all this business, Ian,' Mr Cooper pleaded. 'You're on another wild-goose chase, like that coal-scuttle affair. Can't you go and look quietly at your stamps or something?'

'No, Dad. I'm sure I'm on the trail of our car. Let's tell the police about the Glovers.'

'But we haven't any real evidence, Ian. Only suspicions. And it doesn't sound as if Mr Glover was the man who took my car. The description doesn't tally. You say Mr Glover had dark hair, but the thief——'

'Dad, did someone else see your car taken?'

'The police found a witness. A typist in the office overlooking the place where I park the car. She remembers seeing a man in a white overall coat unlock my Mini and drive it away. She thought he was from our works because many of our chaps do wear white overalls.'

'What time was the car stolen, Dad?'

'Soon after half past eleven, as near as the girl could remember.'

'Then Mr Glover could have been the man in

the white coat. He took it off before he passed
me, of course.'

'And changed the number plates, Ian ? ' Mr
Cooper shook his head. ' I don't think the times
fit. He couldn't have changed the plates in town
or somebody would have seen him, and probably
reported the incident to the police. He must have
driven to a quiet spot outside the town to change
the plates, and then back to his house. I doubt if
he could have done that and passed you when
he did.'

' It's *possible*, Dad.'

' Yes, but there's another detail. The man who
took my car had fair hair, and you said Mr Glover's
was dark.'

' I'm pretty sure it was, Dad.'

Mrs Cooper confirmed this. ' I remember Mr
Glover had dark hair, but he was almost bald
on top.'

' Perhaps he wore a wig for the car theft,' Ian
suggested, persisting doggedly in his suspicions.
' It could have been part of his disguise, like the
white coat.'

Mr Cooper remained unconvinced. ' I don't
see why he would go to all that trouble to steal
our Mini, Ian. Nor would any car thief, for that
matter. No, no. It's almost certain our Mini has
been driven to London. It was probably taken
by a member of a London gang. The typist saw
the car turn into the London road and the police
are also pretty sure that's where it has gone. To
look for a stolen car in London is like looking for
a needle in a haystack.'

'The police didn't think our Mini might have been taken to use in a payroll snatch?' Ian asked.

'They never mentioned that. But they did tell me that a lot of cars are being stolen now for selling on the Continent. There's quite a flourishing underground market. The registration numbers are altered, of course, and false registration books made out. Then the cars are driven abroad by members of the gang posing as holiday-makers. They take the cars by sea or air. I'm afraid that's where our new Mini has gone, Ian.'

'Oh, dear!' Mrs Cooper sighed. 'And apart from the loss of the car our holidays will be spoilt now. Whatever shall we do about them, Paul?'

Mr Cooper shrugged and looked more gloomy than ever. 'We must forget about them, I'm afraid. At least, about camping on the Continent. We'll have to make do with a day at Brighton, by the look of things.'

'Unless we get our car back in time, Dad,' Ian said. 'I wish you'd come to the police with me and tell them about the Glovers.'

'No!' Mr Cooper banged his fist on the table. 'I've told you you're on a wild-goose chase, Ian. Now drop it. I don't want to hear another word about the Glovers, and I'm sure the police don't need your help. They're not likely to listen to you after that coal-scuttle business.'

'But, Dad——'

'Drop it, I say, Ian. Isn't it enough for me to have all this worry about the car without you plaguing me with your absurd theories?'

'Very well, Dad.' Ian sighed a long-suffering

sigh and then remained silent. But not for long.
A thought struck him. ' Dad, if I should happen
to find our car by any chance . . .'

' Well ? '

' Will you forget about that scratch on the door ?
About stopping my pocket money, I mean ? '

Mr Cooper smiled. ' All right, it's a deal. But
I'm afraid we've seen the last of our Mini.'

' I'm not so sure, Dad.'

Ian finished his tea quickly and prepared to
go out.

' Hey, where are you off to in such a hurry,
Ian ? ' Mr Cooper asked. ' You're not going to
do anything stupid, I hope ? You're not going to
the police on your own ? '

' Oh, no, Dad. As you say, they probably
wouldn't listen to me. I'm going round to Roy's.'

' Oh, that's all right.'

If Mr Cooper had known what was going on in
Ian's mind at that moment he would not have
looked so reassured. For Ian had decided that
everything was up to him now. He must battle
on alone. Somehow he must find the evidence to
lay the Glovers by the heels, and that could only
be done by more detective work.

Ian explained the position to Roy, adding, ' I'm
going along to keep watch on that house in Beech
Close. I don't suppose you feel like coming ? '

' Well, I don't mind. You need someone sen-
sible to keep an eye on you, Ian, and it's a nice
evening.'

' Hullo, what's happened to change your opin-
ions, Roy ? ' Ian looked suspiciously at his

friend's freckled face, which was a sphynx-like mask.

' Happened ? ' Roy inquired blandly.

' I thought you were like Dad, certain I'm on a wild-goose chase.'

' You probably are.'   Roy gave Ian a friendly punch.   ' All the same, I'll string along with you, just to keep you from doing something foolhardy.'

As the boys set off on their bicycles Ian questioned Roy again.

' Has your dad been home, Roy ?   Have you talked to him about the Glovers ? '

' He did nip in for a quick cup of tea,' Roy admitted.   ' I didn't have much chance to talk to him though.'

' But he must have said something, or you wouldn't be coming along with me now.'

' Well, I did find out that he's working on the case of your car, Ian.   Dad thinks it's gone to London, and will be taken to the Continent for selling.'

' What else did you find out ? '

' Nothing more from Dad.   But I happened to mention to Mum that we'd been to Beech Close and it turns out she knows someone who knows the Glovers.'

' Well ? '

' Mum says the Glovers have only rented that house furnished for a few months, Ian.   They've told the neighbours they're home on holiday from Africa.'

Ian whistled.   ' A likely story ! '

' Mum thinks they've been in that house about two months.'

'Long enough to case the joint. Now they're going into action.'

'Maybe.' Roy shrugged. 'We've no proof yet, mind.'

'We'll get it. We *must* get it, Roy.'

'If we can manage to see the engine number of that Mini it might help.'

'Yes, and we'll have a jolly good try to inspect the Glovers' Mini. If it is their Mini.'

'You know the number of your father's engine?'

'Of course. I've made a note of all the gen.'

When they reached Beech Close Louise was not about.

'Probably her bed-time,' Roy commented. 'The Glovers don't seem to be here either.'

'Perhaps they're not back yet. Go and ring their bell, Roy.'

'No thanks. That's your job. You've got your cover story all ready and you're good at spinning yarns.'

'Coward!' Ian taunted.

He went to the front door and rang the bell. Then, as there was no answer, he tried the back door. The second ring was perfunctory, as he saw that the garage was still empty.

The side door was tempting and Ian could not resist slipping inside the garage for another quick look round. But he did not discover any fresh clues. He went back to Roy.

The boys cycled back to the telephone box opposite Beech Close and sat on the broad grass verge, pretending to be idling away the evening and watching cars.

Ian raised the bonnet

Watching cars they certainly were, waiting for a mauve Mini. They sat there for quite a time, and in the end their patience was rewarded. A mauve Mini came along the road from the town and turned into Beech Close. It was being driven by Mrs Glover, a smart-looking woman with short cropped blonde hair. Mr Glover was in the other front seat. He appeared much neater than when Ian had first seen him, for he now wore a white shirt with a tie, and his bulky shoulders were not so conspicuous.

' I didn't notice a scratch on the passenger door, Ian,' Roy said.

' Neither did I,' Ian agreed. ' But then, this may be the Glovers' Mini. Either they've got rid of ours and come back in theirs, or they've come back in ours with their number plates on. We've got to find out.'

Roy produced a penny. ' Heads it is, tails it isn't,' he said lightly.

' Oh, don't fool about, Roy. How are we going to get a look at that engine number ? '

' You can try your idea of offering to wash the car.'

' All right. Come and give me a hand.'

Roy grumbled, but agreed. They gave the Glovers a few minutes to settle down, then went to the house. The mauve Mini was on the drive, in front of the closed garage doors.

Mr Glover answered Ian's ring.

' Hullo, lad. What can I do for you ? ' Mr Glover's manner surprised Ian by its geniality. Did the good mood spring from a successful business deal on the thieves' market ?

' Well, it's like this . . .' Ian spun his yarn about wanting to earn some extra pocket money for his holiday.

Mr Glover took it with great good humour. He waved Ian to the car.

' Certainly, my lad. I'll get you a bucket. Just wash the dust off—I'll do the polishing later. Matter of fact the car could do with a wash down because we've just come back from London.'

' Oh ? ' Ian looked at the car. It was certainly dusty.

' Yes, my wife went up by train this morning. I joined her this afternoon and we came back together.'

' I see. You couldn't manage to drive up this morning ? '

' No. I had to be here because I was expecting a business phone call. Now, just a tick while I get you a bucket from the garage and show you where the tap is. Oh, you've a friend outside the gate ? '

' Yes, he'll help me.'

Ian beckoned to Roy, who came up without any show of enthusiasm. The two boys began their task of washing the Mini, and after making sure they were getting on with the job all right Mr Glover left them.

' I'm just going to have a bite to eat, lads,' he called back. ' Ring the bell when you've finished.'

' Goody ! ' Ian murmured to Roy. ' Now's our chance.'

The moment Mr Glover had entered the house and closed the door Ian slipped back the catch and raised the bonnet to check the engine number.

CHAPTER 5

STARTLING NEWS

IAN had made notes in his diary of the particulars of his father's Mini, but did not need to refer to them. The number on the engine block was certainly a strange one.

'So this *is* the Glovers' Mini, Roy.' Ian closed the bonnet. 'Disappointing, but just what I really expected. They've sold our Mini somewhere, and come back in theirs.'

'You may be right,' Roy said cautiously. 'If you are it's going to be an awful job to get any proof that they stole your Mini.'

'But we *will* get proof, Roy,' Ian retorted with grim determination. 'We will get proof—and good enough proof to make your father listen.'

'I don't see how.' Roy shrugged. 'Anyway, I suppose we've got to finish this washing job now that you've let us in for it.'

'Yes, and while we're busy we'll keep our eyes open for clues.'

'Clues? What else is there to find? You've looked at the door and it isn't scratched. You've checked the engine number. What else do you expect to discover?'

'Almost anything,' Ian answered vaguely, stooping for another close look at the door. There was no trace of a scratch on it. 'In particular, Roy,

we must look for the spare number plates—the
ones they used for our Mini.'

'Another set bearing these numbers?' Roy
sponged over the front number plate.

'It's the number of the car we saw at lunch-
time, Roy.'

'Yes, and these plates can't have been taken off
recently. Look, the paint on the bolts hasn't been
disturbed.'

'There you are, Roy! A clue!'

'Hm, I don't see it proves anything.'

'Of course it does. It means there must be
another set of these number plates. I bet the
Glovers brought the duplicates back with them,
ready to use again.'

'Maybe the plates are still in the car, Ian.
Have a look in the boot.'

'It's probably locked.' Ian glanced at the
windows of the house. No-one seemed to be
watching, so he went round to the back of the
Mini. The boot was not locked, but it was
empty.

'Try inside the car,' Roy suggested. 'Pretend
to be washing the windows. We'll do a thorough
job while we're at it.'

'We certainly will.' Ian grinned and took the
washleather.

While making a show of wiping the windows Ian
searched in the parcel spaces and odd corners.
All he found were a few paper shopping bags from
an Oxford Street store. They were lying openly
on the back seat.

He peeped into them. They contained dress

materials, and a blouse. Two of the bags had receipts in them, bearing the day's date.

'Looks as if Mrs Glover has been to London, Roy.' Ian reported his discoveries. 'I wonder what she was really doing up there.'

'Establishing an alibi? She had to get this Mini out of the way today, to leave the coast clear for her husband to pinch yours. So she drove to London in it and went shopping. Later, if Mr Glover really did take your Mini, Ian, he drove it up to London and flogged it to his crooked pals, then met his wife and they came home in this one.'

'Could be.' Ian nodded. 'It all fits together. And Mr Glover must have driven our Mini to London with false number plates on. Now, if we could find those plates . . .'

'Or find where Mrs Glover parked her car, and prove that it was in London while her husband was driving about here in a Mini with the same number plates. That would be awkward for them, Ian.' Roy paused, and his old caution returned. 'But we may be barking up the wrong tree, like you did in that antique——'

'I'm sure I'm not,' Ian interrupted impatiently. 'You saw the scratch on that Mini at lunch time.'

'Yes, but it wasn't a bad one. Suppose Mr Glover did manage to polish it out before he drove up to meet his wife? This *could* be the same one.'

'I'm sure he didn't. This is a different car.'

Roy stood back and surveyed the Mini. 'If it's the same car then Mrs Glover must have gone to London by train. Louise said the Glovers went out in their car after breakfast this morning. Mr Glover could have taken his wife to the station.'

Ian shook his head. ' She drove up to London in this Mini, Roy. Somehow we've got to prove it. If we can find a few witnesses—suppose we ask at all the garages on the London road ? She may have stopped for petrol.'

' That's not likely, if she was covering her tracks,' Roy said.

The boys were putting the finishing touches to their work when Mrs Glover came out. She looked cool and neat in a summer dress. Her short blonde hair was golden in the evening sunlight. She smiled at them.

' Hullo, boys. Have you finished ? '

They nodded.

' Good. Now, what are your names ? '

They told her. Mrs Glover looked curiously at Ian.

' Oh, you're Mrs Cooper's son.' Mrs Glover's smile became even more friendly. ' I know your mother quite well, Ian, but I haven't met you before. My husband tells me you're doing odd jobs because you want to earn some pocket money for your holiday.'

' That's right.'

' Where are you going on holiday, Ian ? '

' To France—I hope.'

' Why the doubt ? '

' We had planned a motoring tour.' Ian watched her face. ' But our car's been stolen and we may not be able to go.'

' Stolen ? Your Mini ? ' Mrs Glover appeared

to be startled by the news. 'How awful! You had a mauve Mini like this one, didn't you?'

'Just like it.' Ian nodded.

'The Coopers' Mini was stolen just before lunch today, Mrs Glover,' Roy said.

'Oh, where from?'

'The park outside Mr Cooper's works.'

'I see. Have the police found any clues?'

'A few.' Ian spoke quickly, thinking bluff might be useful to shake the cool confidence Mrs Glover was showing. 'I expect they'll get the thieves in the end.'

'I hope they do,' Mrs Glover said. 'I daresay somebody took it for a joy ride, Ian. It'll probably be found abandoned somewhere before long.'

'The police have another theory, Mrs Glover,' Ian hinted darkly. 'I'm afraid we may not see our Mini again. It's probably in London by now, even on its way to the Continent.'

'Really?' Mrs Glover flicked a speck of dust from her dress. 'You mean thieves are stealing cars for selling abroad?'

'Yes. By the way, Mrs Glover, I believe you were up in London today. I don't suppose you happened to see a mauve Mini that might have been ours? I mean, if you went up by road you may have seen——'

'I didn't go by road, Ian.' Mrs Glover cut him short. 'I went by train—and that reminds me, you can take a message to your mother for me. Tell her I travelled up with Mrs Barlow this morning and we discussed the next play for the Townswomen's Guild. We'll call round tomorrow and see your mother about it.'

Ian said he would pass the message on, and wondered if it had been made up on the spur of the moment by Mrs Glover. Had his curiosity made her uneasy ? Had she become suspicious ?

But Mrs Glover did not betray any signs of uneasiness as she paid the boys and saw them to the gate. Mr Glover did not come out again.

At the corner of Beech Close Ian stopped. ' I know Mrs Barlow, Roy. Let's call on her and check.'

' You think Mrs Glover was trying to pull wool over our eyes with that talk of going to London by train ? '

' Of course.'

Roy shook his head. ' Mrs Glover wouldn't make up a story like that, knowing we could check it. I believe she *did* go to London by train, Ian.'

' I don't—and if we can prove it, Roy, will you get your dad to listen to my theories ? '

' All right, it's a deal.'

' Goody ! ' Ian grinned and led the way to Mrs Barlow's house, but there his hopes were dashed.

' Oh, yes, Ian dear,' Mrs Barlow said, ' I did see Mrs Glover this morning. We travelled to London together.'

' By train ? '

' Yes. We got to the station at the same time, as it happened. Mr Glover had driven her in their car and they arrived at the station just as I was stepping off my bus.'

' Mr Glover drove away again ? ' Ian asked.

' Yes, at once. Mrs Glover told me he had to stay at home over lunch-time as he was expecting an important telephone call, but that he would be driving up to London later on, to meet her. I remember Mrs Glover saying she was glad she wouldn't have to carry her parcels home.'

Mrs Barlow also remembered the play they had discussed on the train. She gave Ian a message about it for his mother.

Ian was disappointed. Mrs Glover's alibi seemed perfect. She *had* gone to London by train that morning. She *had* shopped in Oxford Street.

'And that means Mr Glover was driving their Mini when we saw him at lunch-time,' Roy pointed out as they cycled home. 'The scratch you saw on the door must have been a dust mark more than anything, Ian, and he polished it off before he went to London. You've made a mountain out of a molehill, just as you did with that antique coal-scuttle business. I'm jolly glad I didn't say anything to Dad about your wild theories.'

'They're not wild theories,' Ian insisted stubbornly. 'Mrs Glover went to London, by train, I grant you, but that still leaves him free. He could have hidden their Mini somewhere quite close and then stolen Dad's car.'

'What about the London trip, Ian? The Glovers drove back from London in their car this evening.'

'Suppose Mr Glover parked his Mini at that small town a couple of stops up the line, then nipped back here by train to steal ours?' Ian theorised. 'Then, this evening he came back by train with Mrs Glover as far as that, and picked up their Mini to drive home. We ought to check all garages and car parks in that town, and at other places up the main line, but it would be a big job. Needs police help. Roy, you must tell your father.'

'Certainly not. He'll only blame me for wasting his time. Oh, no, Ian. I'm not luring Dad in on this now. I don't think you've got a case. It's all "suppose this" and "suppose that". We haven't a shred of proof.'

Ian cycled on in a brooding silence for a time. Then he brightened as a plan came to him.

'Tell you what, Roy. I'm going to have a shot at searching the Glovers' garage thoroughly to-morrow.'

'After school? How will you do that?'

'Simple. I'll get Mother to ask them round to tea. That will get them out of the way and we can search the garage on our way home from school. I bet we find the duplicate number plates there.'

'I bet we don't,' Roy retorted with conviction. 'You can count me out of your mad scheme. I'm not going to have anything to do with it.'

'Oh, yes, you are. At least you can keep watch outside for me while I'm searching the garage. I may be some time.'

Roy repeated that he would have nothing to do with such a scheme. He could imagine it ending in horrible embarrassment. His ears turned red at the very thought.

Ian kept on trying to persuade him, not only that evening, but the next morning when they rode to school, and during the morning break. There were moments when Roy seemed to weaken, when he listened sympathetically to Ian's reminders of how they had always been friends and helped one another, but then he would think of the embarrassing possibilities if anything went wrong.

He was still being stubborn when they cycled home to lunch, but on the way an errand boy they knew stopped them. He was bursting with news.

'Say, Ian, have you heard about the payroll snatch? The crooks used a mauve Mini for their getaway—I reckon it was your dad's car.'

CHAPTER 6

BOB'S STORY

IAN nearly fell off his bicycle and Roy was so startled he collided with the errand boy's front wheel.

'Where was this, Bob?' Ian asked.

'When was it?' Roy queried eagerly.

'What happened?'

'Well, the snatch was made from Brown's van, just before it got back to their factory from the bank with an extra big load of cash. Brown's will shut down this Friday, you know, for their annual fortnight's holiday, so there was double the usual amount of money in the van.'

'Brown's!' Ian whistled. 'That's a big factory. The crooks must have got several thousand pounds.'

Bob nodded. 'And they must have planned the grab carefully. They must have had plenty of local knowledge. They knew this was the day to get the holiday payroll, and they did the job in Quarry Lane, the narrow, quiet bit just before the factory.'

'What's this about a mauve Mini, Bob?' Roy asked.

'The bandits used one for the job. It was parked across Quarry Lane, blocking it. When the van turned into the lane it had to stop, and before the men in the van had time to reverse or do anything they were attacked by men wearing gas masks. The bandits tossed tear-gas bombs into the van.'

'Tear gas!' Ian exclaimed.

'Yes. The men in the van were put out of action and the bandits took the cash without trouble. They made off towards the London Road in the Mini.'

'How many bandits were there, Bob?' Roy asked.

'Two.'

'Men, you said?' Ian queried.

'That's right.' Bob nodded again. 'They weren't in the Mini. They were hiding in the bushes at the side of the lane, one on each side. They pounced on the van like lightning. It was a proper ambush.'

'I know the lane,' Roy said. 'The bushes offer useful cover. But how did the bandits know the van would use the lane?'

'It always does.' Bob shrugged. 'Quarry Lane is the shortest way to the factory. The only other approach is from the by-pass and that's miles round.'

'Brown's are like a lot of other firms, I suppose,' Ian said. 'They've got slack about precautions against bandits.'

'You know, Ian,' Bob continued, 'I reckon it was your dad's Mini they used for the job. They stole it yesterday so as to have it ready. I wonder where they hid it last night?'

'So do I.' Ian brightened. His holiday might yet be saved.

If the Mini used for the payroll grab was his father's, then it would almost certainly have been abandoned somewhere close to the town, when the bandits transferred to another car to complete their getaway.

Ian asked Bob more questions, but his supply of facts was almost exhausted. The only other point of importance Ian discovered was that the grab had been made shortly after ten that morning.

'The van was waiting at the bank when it opened,' Bob explained. 'The money was loaded in and then the van nipped off back to the factory —and ran into the ambush in Quarry Lane. The grab was a smart job, I must say, and if you ask me it's that big London gang. The one who did that wages grab at Wimbledon a fortnight ago, and the London Airport job the week before that.'

'Maybe.' Ian prepared to move off. When it came to theorising he didn't need to listen to Bob's suggestions. He had plenty of theories of his own. But if Bob was right about the London gang then the Glovers were surely part of it.

More boys came along and the talkative Bob began to tell his news all over again. Ian and Roy left him and rode to the corner where they usually parted.

'This certainly makes things look different, Ian,' Roy admitted, but with a trace of his customary caution. 'You think the Glovers are something to do with that London gang?'

'Yes. I bet they're the gang's spies. They found out all the local gen.'

'It's possible.　They've been here long enough.'

'Mr Glover may even be the master mind of the gang.　Anyway, he must have had something to do with the car plans and that ambush—and we're too late now to catch him.'

'Too late?'

'Well, you don't suppose the Glovers are still at their house in Beech Close, do you, Roy?　They'll have bunked.　Mr Glover was probably one of the men who did the actual grab.'

'Oh.'

'We must tell your father, Roy.　Will he be home to lunch?'

'I doubt it.　He'll be busy on the robbery.'

'Then we must phone him.　It's urgent.'

Roy considered, fidgeting on his bicycle at the corner.　'Tell you what, let's see if Dad comes home to lunch.　If not we'll phone.'

'No, let's phone now.　There's a box just along the road.'

Roy was none too keen, but Ian insisted.　They parked their bicycles at the phone box and squeezed inside.　Roy had begun to dial when Ian interrupted.

'Look, Roy!'

A mauve Mini was approaching.　The number was that of the Glovers' car and as it passed Ian saw that Mrs Glover was driving.　She was alone.

Roy replaced the telephone.　'You were wrong about the Glovers having done a bunk, Ian.　She's on her way home to lunch.'

'Of all the nerve!' Ian exclaimed.　'They're certainly playing it cool, but that doesn't make any difference to phoning your dad, Roy. Get cracking again.'

Roy did as he was bid, reluctantly. He wasn't encouraged when he got through to his father and was greeted with a gruff, impatient voice.

' Well, Roy ? What is it ? Why are you phoning me ? You know I've told you——'

' Sorry, Dad, but it's about this payroll snatch.'

' Oh ? '

' Is it true a mauve Mini was used by the gang ? '

' That's right. The one belonging to Ian's father. Two people got the number as it made off. Why ? Have you seen it ? '

' No, Dad, but Ian thinks he knows who stole it.'

' Ian does ? ' There was a pause, followed by a muttered, ' Then heaven help us ! '

' Listen, Dad. It's like this . . .' Roy launched into an explanation, helped by Ian, who put in his theories.

Detective Sergeant Kenton listened with some impatience and incredulity and presently broke in.

' I think you're barking up the wrong tree again, Ian. As a matter of fact we already know about the Glovers and their mauve Mini.'

' Ah, so they're under suspicion ! '

' Nothing of the kind, Ian. It just happens that after the payroll grab this morning we searched the town for the mauve Mini, expecting to find it abandoned. We haven't found the car yet, but we did come across a mauve Mini in the car park opposite the church. It was locked, and the attendant was telling us about Mrs Glover when she came along. I spoke to her and she said she was in the town for coffee and shopping, which I gather is her normal morning routine. The car-park attendant confirmed this.'

' A phoney story, sir,' Ian said, without hesitation. ' What time did she park the Mini ? '

' Shortly before the raid. We checked the ticket, purely from routine. The payroll van was ambushed in Quarry Lane at ten minutes past ten, or just after. Mrs Glover parked her Mini at five past ten.'

' All right, sir. That leaves her in the clear. But I bet Mr Glover was in our Mini doing the grab with another member of the gang.'

' You're wrong, Ian. He was with his wife in the car when they parked.'

' Oh.'

For the first time since hearing Bob's news of the ambush Ian's certainty that he was on the track of the payroll gang wavered.

Seeing Mrs Glover driving home in her Mini had given Ian a momentary jolt, but not a serious one. He thought she was bluffing. Playing it cool to disarm suspicion. But now . . . Could he be making a terrible mistake ?

' I think you'd better forget about the Glovers, Ian,' Mr Kenton advised. ' Thank you all the same for your information.'

' But the Glovers *could* have planned the payroll grab, sir.' Ian clung to his theories. ' Where is he now ? She was alone in the car when she passed this box on her way home a minute ago.'

' Oh, was she ? '

'Yes, sir. I bet he's already bunked and she's going to pull out pretty soon.'

Mr Kenton laughed. 'You never let go once you get your teeth into a suspect, do you, Ian ? '

'Not when the suspect has stolen our car and probably ruined my summer holiday, sir. Mrs Glover may have a good alibi for yesterday morning, but what about Mr Glover ? Where was he at the time our car was stolen ? '

'Hm. We didn't ask about the Glovers' movements yesterday, Ian.'

'I should have told you about my discoveries sooner, Mr Kenton. I wanted Roy to tell you, but he wouldn't. Neither would Dad.'

'A case of once bitten twice shy.' Mr Kenton chuckled. 'And you haven't any real evidence, not even a clue if it comes to that.'

'Except for the scratch on the car Mr Glover was driving yesterday. I'm certain it was our Mini.'

'The scratch may have been a dust mark, as Roy says.'

Ian maintained that it was the real scratch. He begged Mr Kenton to arrest the Glovers (if they could still be found) and to search the house in Beech Close. But Mr Kenton would stress the lack of evidence, and he reminded Ian there was such a thing as coincidence.

'I'm sure it isn't coincidence, sir. I find it very suspicious that Mr Glover wasn't with his wife just now when she drove home.'

Mr Kenton sighed. 'You think he's already made his getaway ? But if so Mrs Glover would surely have gone with him. No, you must be wrong. Now, get along home to lunch, both of you, or you'll be late. I'll—oh, hold on a second.'

There was a murmur of voices and then silence as Mr Kenton covered the mouthpiece of his telephone. To the waiting boys it seemed a long time before his voice came again.

' Hullo, Ian. You still there ? '

' Yes, sir.'

' We've just had a report that your car's been found. Thought you'd like to know.'

' Found ! Where, sir ? '

' In Wimbledon. It was abandoned in a " no waiting " area. It seems to be all right, so your holiday should be safe, after all.'

' That's something. Any clues in the car, sir ? '

' The C.I.D. are going over it now. The crash helmets and gas masks were found in the car, but not the bags in which the cash had been stowed.'

' So the bandits made their getaway almost to London in the Mini, Dad ? ' Roy broke in. ' They didn't change cars ? '

' Evidently not. They scooted through, and evaded our patrols. It would have been too dangerous to go right into London, of course. They had a nerve to go as far as they did in the Mini, knowing that the alarm must have been raised very soon after the ambush.'

' I hope the C.I.D. find Mr Glover's finger prints,' Ian said. ' I wonder where he hid our car last night ? '

' If *he* hid it,' Mr Kenton retorted.

' Of course he did.' Ian felt certain on that

point. ' He drove it to London, or close to London, and parked it with another member of the gang. Under false number plates, of course.'

' That theory doesn't fit, Ian. I've got the mileage reading here, and the one your father gave me. Your father was certain about the mileage he'd done because he made a note of it yesterday morning after filling up with petrol. The figure on the clock now shows that the car hasn't been driven much farther than from here to Wimbledon. Certainly not up there for the night and then down again for the raid. Your Mini must have been hidden quite close to the town, Ian.'

CHAPTER 7

THE ALIBI

' WELL, Ian. That hits all your theories for six.'
Roy sounded relieved as they left the box.

' I'm not so sure,' Ian retorted.

' You don't *still* think the Glovers are mixed up
in the payroll snatch ? '

' I've got a hunch they are.'

Roy groaned. ' So you're not giving up ? '

' Certainly not. Now, the next thing to do is
to search their garage. I'll ask Mum to have Mrs
Glover to tea this afternoon.'

' And Mr Glover ? '

' Included in the invitation, of course—if he's
at home.'

The boys separated for lunch. Ian burst in on
his mother with an excited account of the payroll
robbery, only to find out that she already knew
the story.

' Roy's father rang me up a minute or two ago,
Ian,' Mrs Cooper explained. ' He told me our
Mini has been recovered. The police will bring
it back to us when they've finished looking for
finger prints and so on. Isn't it a relief to know that
it's safe ? Now we shall be able to go camping in
France as we planned.'

Ian steered the conversation round artlessly to
the subject of the tea invitation, but his mother
failed to rise to his hints with any sense of urgency.

' Oh, it would be too short notice today, Ian dear. Next week will be time enough to ask the Glovers round.'

' But from what Mrs Glover said last night, Mum, I think she wants to see you about this play she mentioned.'

' We've already discussed it.'

' You've seen Mrs Glover this morning, Mum ? '

' Yes, we had coffee together in the café by the roundabout.'

' Had you arranged to meet Mrs Glover there ? '

' No. I was having coffee by myself when she walked in.'

' What time was that ? '

' Oh, about half past ten.'

Ian ate in silence for a while, considering. Mr and Mrs Glover had parked their Mini in the town at about five minutes past ten. Then she had arrived alone at the café at half past ten. What had they been doing in the meantime, and what had become of Mr Glover ?

' Did Mrs Glover say where her husband was, Mum ? '

' He was shopping. She said he can't stand women chattering over morning coffee, so he wouldn't come with her.'

' How long did you chatter to Mrs Glover ? '

' Just an hour, Ian. You see, we were busy talking about this play and the time simply flew. I didn't realise how late it was until I heard the church clock strike half past eleven. Then, of course, I had to fly.'

' What did Mrs Glover do ? '

'She left the café with me and we parted outside.'

'If you had so much to talk about I should think you ought to have her to tea today, Mum. I mean, you can't have finished settling all the details about that play?'

'Why are you so keen to ask the Glovers to tea all of a sudden?' Mrs Cooper looked at Ian shrewdly. 'There must be something behind all this?'

'Oh, just interest, Mum. Just interest.' Ian waved a hand in a vague gesture. 'The Glovers seemed friendly yesterday evening and I thought I'd like to see a bit more of them, 'specially as their home's in Africa. I wouldn't mind going to Africa when I leave school.'

Mrs Cooper gave her son a long thoughtful look as she picked up his empty plate.

'Well, if it's Africa you're thinking about I'll see if the Glovers can come to tea one day next week.'

And with that most unsatisfactory pronouncement Ian had to be content. He could not do more without rousing acute suspicion.

He sat thinking dark thoughts about how awkward grown-ups could be. They were difficult to steer at times. Obstinate as donkeys.

Ian was jolted out of his mooning by the arrival of his father in a police car with Detective Sergeant Kenton.

'Hullo, Ian.' Roy's father smiled cheerily and put down the case he was carrying on a chair. 'Any more clues for me?'

' Er no, sir.', Ian was taken aback by the sudden arrival of the detective. Then the thought that the police might want help after all cheered Ian. ' But if you want to know more about the Glovers I can tell you——'

Mr Kenton cut Ian short with a laugh. ' No, I don't want to hear more of your fanciful theories, my lad. Anyway, the Glovers are in the clear. They have an alibi for the time of the robbery. Besides, the car being abandoned in Wimbledon suggests that it was the big London gang who did the job.'

' But the Glovers could be part of the gang, sir. Perhaps Mr Glover is the boss of the gang.'

Mr Cooper frowned at Ian. ' That's enough of your chatter, my lad. Mr Kenton didn't come here to listen to your wild ideas. He wants your finger prints.'

' My finger prints, Dad ? '

' Yes, he's already taken mine. He'll want your mother's prints too.'

' Just for checking with any prints found on the car,' Mr Kenton explained. ' We must be able to eliminate the finger prints of the family, you see.'

Mr Kenton opened his case and took out an inking pad and paper.

Ian enjoyed the rather messy business and was sorry when Mr Kenton hurried away afterwards.

Mr Cooper sat down to lunch. He was pleased at the thought of getting his car back, but also worried by the bad treatment it had suffered.

' I'm afraid, Ian, that as the gangsters used it for their getaway car they'll have driven it flat out, and the engine isn't fully run-in. I do hope they haven't damaged it.'

' They don't seem to have driven her far, Dad,' Ian said consolingly.

' No, but if she was harshly treated for those miles the valves may have warped, or the bores been damaged.'

Mrs Cooper insisted on looking on the bright side. ' Don't fuss so, Paul. We've got the car back in time for our holiday and that's what really matters.'

Ian felt that the important thing was to find out who had stolen the Mini, but he did not say anything. When he met Roy after lunch he had to confess that his hopes for the afternoon had been dashed.

' Still, we'll go along to Beech Close and hope for the best, Roy. The Glovers may be out—or they may have cleared off altogether by then. Have you heard anything more about the payroll grab ? '

' No. Dad didn't come home.'

That afternoon lessons seemed to Ian to drag deplorably. The hands of the clock on the class-room wall had surely never moved so slowly ? But when he was free and had reached Beech Close with Roy the impatience of the afternoon was proved useless. The Glovers were at home. Very much so. They were both in the front of the house. Mrs Glover was weeding a flower bed. Her husband was polishing the Mini. It stood on the drive before the open garage doors.

Ian did not approach within range, but surveyed

the scene from half way along Beech Close, where a tree made a useful screen.

' Foiled ! ' Ian exclaimed bitterly. ' They'll be busy for hours. We'd better go home to tea and try again later.'

' What about checking the Glovers' alibi with the car-park attendant ? ' Roy suggested. ' The times Dad mentioned seemed pretty close. I wonder if there's something to be found there ? '

' Good idea,' Ian agreed. ' It won't take long to go to the car park and I know Old Charlie. He's mostly there, giving out the tickets.'

' Yes, I know him too. He's a bit sour if you don't catch him in the right mood.'

' I hope he's in a good mood today. The sun's warm, and he likes that. It's in winter you have to watch your step with him.'

They cycled into the town and found Old Charlie sunning himself on a seat outside the little wooden hut which acted as his shelter and office. The rush of the day was over and he was in a relaxed mood.

After a suitable time spent talking about the weather, cricket and football prospects for the next season, Old Charlie was steered to the subject of the mauve Mini.

' Oh, yes, of course I know the car, and Mrs Glover. Nice woman. Comes 'ere as regular as clockwork. Mr Glover's often with 'er too, and 'e's a good one for yarnin' to you about Africa. Good as one of those television programmes 'e is. Why, last week 'e was tellin' me——'

' Yes.' Ian broke in hastily on Old Charlie's

rambling before he started repeating tales of Africa. ' What I'd like to know is the time Mrs Glover parked here this morning.'

' Ah ! That's what the police asked. Because she 'as a mauve car like the one as done the raid. Why do you want to know the same thing ? Are you playing at being detectives ? '

Ian admitted that he was, and was relieved when Old Charlie took him seriously.

' Yes, well, you might jump to conclusions like,' Old Charlie admitted. ' That is if you didn't know Mrs Glover. But she's all right, and comes into the town as regular as clockwork for 'er mornin' coffee.'

' What time did she park this morning ? '

' Just after ten.'

' How much after, exactly ? '

' Five minutes. That's what I wrote on 'er ticket. She was a bit late, really, because she's usually in by ten. She's told me afore now as she likes to be 'ere by ten because after ten it's difficult to find a place in the summer.'

' How do you tell the time ? '

' By the church clock, of course.' Old Charlie pointed to the stone tower opposite. The clock face could be read clearly from the car park.

' Oh, I see. And that would be the right time ? '

' Yes. Always the right time. Good as Big Ben that clock. I goes by it all day. No need of a watch 'ere.'

' And you write the time on the ticket when a car comes in ? '

' That's the system, lad. You pay by the hour,

see, so it's important to put the time on the ticket. I'm always most particular about putting the proper time.'

A few cars came into the park while the boys were talking to Old Charlie and they saw the system in operation. Whenever he wrote a ticket Old Charlie glanced up at the church clock and put down the exact time.

'The clock's certainly O.K. by my watch, Ian,' Roy said, while Old Charlie was busy with a car. 'That alibi of the Glovers is as sound as a bell.'

Ian wrinkled his nose. 'Good detectives always suspect alibis that are sound.'

When Old Charlie was free again Ian asked him what time Mrs Glover had left the park that morning.

'A quarter past twelve. I remember particularly, because she should 'ave paid for an extra 'our by rights, but I let 'er off with the charge for two 'ours, seein' as she'd been 'eld up a bit by the police when they was 'ere askin' questions.'

Ian nodded. That fitted with the time when she had driven past the phone box.

'Was Mrs Glover alone then ? '

'Yes. She told me 'er 'usband was walkin' 'ome as 'e needed exercise.'

Ian glanced at Roy. There was surely something odd about the Glovers' movements that morning ? What had Mr Glover been doing ? Had he really walked home ?

Louise might be able to give an answer to the last question. Ian decided to ask her, but first he and Roy went to their homes for their tea.

When they met again, to go to Beech Close, Roy had news.

'Dad looked in for a cup of tea, Ian. He says there weren't any finger prints on your car. It was wiped clean. The crooks must have worn gloves. But there was one clue—scrape marks on the number plates.'

'Scrape marks?'

'Yes. False number plates had been clipped over yours and then removed. The crooks wouldn't have had to fuss with screws. They could clip plates on in a jiffy.'

CHAPTER 8

WEIGHTS

'Dad says they must have been specially made plates, to fit the Mini plates,' Roy continued, as they cycled along. 'With strong springs, of course, and that's why the real number plates were scratched.'

'If Mr Glover used clip-on plates he'd have had ample time to steal our Mini yesterday and be at the corner where he overtook us,' Ian pointed out. 'This makes me more than ever certain he's behind the payroll robbery. I bet those clip-on plates are in his garage, Roy. We *must* search the place.'

They found Louise pushing her dolls' pram up and down her drive. She was talking to the three occupants briskly and when Ian spoke to her she overwhelmed him with chatter about the new dress she had made for the doll which she said was the most beautiful of the three.

By tact and skilful questioning Ian and Roy managed to find out that Mr Glover had not walked home to lunch that day. Louise had seen Mrs Glover return in the car alone. And about an hour later Mrs Glover had gone out again in the car, alone.

'She wasn't away for very long, and when she came back Mr Glover was there too,' Louise said.

'So she fetched him from somewhere?' Ian queried.

'Yes—why? Why are you interested in Mr and Mrs Glover?'

'Oh, I just am. Like I'm interested in dolls.' Ian adroitly checked Louise's curiosity and returned to safer topics.

While he talked of dolls he thought about the mystery of Mr Glover's movements. Had Mr Glover gone off to contact the bandits? Was that why he had 'disappeared' between half past ten and the early afternoon? Had he been making sure that the raid had been successful and that all had gone well with the getaway? Checking that his plans had been carried out?

To Ian's annoyance he saw that the Glovers were still out in the front. They were both gardening now. Really busy. Burying clues, perhaps? Hiding the false number plates in the rose bed whilst pretending to be busy weeding?

Ian mentioned this possibility to Roy, when they had disengaged themselves from the talkative Louise.

'Nonsense, they have to do their gardening sometime, Ian. The garden is very well kept, even though they are only renting the house.'

'Well, I think it's suspicious.'

'Rubbish! You've got into a state where you find everything suspicious. You were wrong about them doing a bunk and I expect you're wrong about them being crooks.'

Ian shook his head stubbornly. 'I've a hunch that I'm on the track of something big.'

Roy groaned. 'A big blunder, most likely.'

'I'm sure there's something wrong with the Glovers' alibi for this morning. Doesn't it strike you that it's pretty close timing ? '

'Well . . . yes.'

'Suppose that church clock had been a quarter of an hour slow, Roy. They *could* have been in Quarry Lane for the raid if that clock was wrong.'

'It's possible.' Roy nodded. 'But they didn't do the snatch, Ian. Two men did the job, and drove off to Wimbledon afterwards.'

'Suppose Mrs Glover had worn trousers. With a jacket and gas mask she could easily have been mistaken for a man.'

'But she was wearing a dress when she parked the car. She can't have done a quick change in that time.'

'She could have put on a jacket and trousers over her dress, Roy. It wouldn't have taken her long to slip them off. The Glovers *could* have done the snatch themselves if that church clock was wrong.'

'But it wasn't wrong. And, apart from that, how do you account for the getaway Mini being found at Wimbledon ? '

'It couldn't have been left there since yesterday, I suppose ? '

'Don't be a chump. It was parked in a busy "no waiting" street. The police would have picked it up very quickly. Besides, it had the gas masks and crash helmets in it, so it had certainly been driven up there immediately after the raid.'

Ian sighed. 'This is like a jig-saw. We've got a jumble of pieces that don't seem to fit, but I bet they do fit. Let's try that alibi again. I wonder if the church clock had been got at?'

'Altered? But you couldn't alter the time on a public clock like that, Ian. Not with people noticing, even if you could get at the mechanism.'

'It wouldn't have had to be altered much. A quarter of an hour would have been enough.'

'If the hands had been altered during the morning people would have seen them move. Somebody would, for sure. Probably Old Charlie himself.'

'But if that clock could have been got at then the Glovers would have an alibi, wouldn't they? And doesn't it strike you that they've been working towards that—I mean, with Mrs Glover establishing a routine of going for coffee most mornings, and all that jazz?'

Roy considered. 'You've a point there, Ian. Mrs Glover did impress herself on Old Charlie, and of course she did know all about the way he wrote out the tickets, and how he was fussy about the time and took it from the church clock.'

Ian picked up his bicycle. 'Come on. Let's investigate that clock.'

They rode into the town and entered the church. Ian was no stranger to the building as he often went to services there on Sundays with his parents. But he had not explored the tower end and now, in the quiet of evening, the empty church seemed strange. He spoke in whispers to Roy.

The tower containing the bells and the clock

was at the west end of the building. A carved wooden screen hung with thick red curtains screened the bellringers' chamber at the base of the tower from the nave.

Ian pushed through the curtains into the dark rectangular room. It was only illuminated by the dim light from the nave coming in above the curtains, where there was a gap of some ten feet between the top of the screen and the ceiling, which was the wooden first floor of the tower. Six bell ropes came through small holes in the ceiling, and were neatly looped back to hooks set in the stone walls close to the boys' heads.

In the silence the ticking of the clock sounded very loud. It was the heartbeat of the tower. Thump . . . thump . . . thump . . .

' It's a pendulum clock, Roy,' Ian remarked. ' Like Big Ben. I've just thought of something.'

' What ? '

' You know Big Ben is regulated by putting pennies (or is it halfpennies ?) into a tray on the pendulum ? Well, suppose the Glovers had managed to hang an extra weight on the pendulum of this clock, to slow it down. That could have given them their alibi, and there wouldn't have been any sudden movement of the hands for people to notice.'

' But the clock would have been wrong this evening,' Roy objected.

' Not if Mr Glover had put it right again—slowly, of course. Perhaps that's what he was doing over lunch-time.'

' But could he get at the clock ? '

' That's what we're going to find out.'

Ian crossed the stone floor to the small door in the corner of the room. He guessed the door opened on to a spiral stone staircase, but when he tried the handle it was locked.

' The key's probably about somewhere,' he told Roy. ' Now, what would be a likely place ? '

' On a nail behind the curtains ? '

The boys searched along the curtains and found the key. Not on a nail, but in a pocket sewn on at one end of the curtains.

Ian unlocked the door.

' Ooh ! It's dark in there, Ian.' Roy drew back. ' I don't fancy going up those stairs. They're like the ones you see in horror films of old castles.'

' Don't be silly. Come on—and shut the door behind you. I've got the key, to make sure we aren't locked in.'

Ian groped his way up the winding stone stair. Faint light from small slit windows did not do much to show them the narrow steps.

At last the boys emerged in the gloom of the clock chamber. The light of one small window was all the illumination, and its leaded panes were thick with cobwebs. The clock mechanism stood in a special frame on one side of the room. Long ropes led from it to massive weights suspended from pulleys in the bell chamber above. Rods and gears drove the hands on the outside clock face. A long pendulum swung slowly to and fro, and seemed somehow menacing as it thudded in the gloom.

He examined the pendulum closely

' Cor ! This gives me the creeps,' Roy muttered nervously.

' Bit spooky, I must say,' Ian agreed. He went up to the pendulum and examined it closely. ' Look here, Roy. The pendulum bob is made of weights. Several of them, and you can take off these top ones quite easily.'

The smaller weights at the top of the pendulum bob were slotted and could be slipped on or off the pile. Ian managed to remove one and replace it without stopping the clock.

While he had the weight off he inspected it closely. There was no dust on it, yet a thick film of dust lay over everything in the clock chamber.

' Here are some more weights, Ian.' Roy found a shelf with spare weights on and was about to pick one up when Ian stopped him.

' Wait ! Maybe the Glovers used those extra weights to slow the clock.'

Ian took out a match and struck it, to get a better look at the weights. There were several sizes, some very small. All but the largest were covered with undisturbed dust, but the heavy one had been moved recently. There was no dust on it, and a track showed on the shelf where it had been dragged off.

' This is it, Roy.' Ian's voice rose with excitement. ' Proof that the clock has been tampered with. Somebody put this weight on the pendulum to slow it down. Then, later on, it was removed and replaced on the shelf.'

' And how was the clock put on to the right time again ? '

'Quite simply. By taking off the weight I removed. It's about the same size as this one.'

'I don't follow, Ian.'

'Look. If this weight is added to the pendulum it will slow the clock, quite quickly too, I should think. Right?'

'Yes.' Roy nodded.

'Well, say that weight took an hour and a half to slow the clock by fifteen minutes. Mr Glover could have nipped up here and put the weight on at half past eight this morning.'

'I see. By ten that would have slowed the clock enough to give them an alibi when they parked the car.'

'Exactly. And having parked the car he nips up here again, takes off the extra weight, and this other weight. That would make the clock speed up. Assuming the weights are the same the clock would regain its proper time in an hour and a half. Then Mr Glover returns this weight to its proper place on the pendulum and everything is O.K. Do you follow?'

'Yes, I do. That means Mr Glover, or Mrs for that matter, made three trips to this clock today. Once early this morning, before the raid. The second time as soon as possible after the raid. Then the third time about an hour and a half after that.'

'You've worked it out. I bet that's what Mr Glover was doing this morning when he wasn't with his wife. He left her when she went to have coffee and he came straight here. He may have stayed here all the while, until the clock was dead right.'

'Could be. But Mrs Glover didn't fetch him until after lunch. That was rather a long time for him to be here.'

'Perhaps it took longer for the clock to regain time than to lose it. Anyway, that's a small point. What we have done is to blow their alibi sky high.'

Ian felt jubilant. But at that moment a loud click and a whirring almost blew him sky high with fright.

His first thought was that the Glovers had found out he was on their trail and come to trap him.

CHAPTER 9

A DISCOVERY

THE unexpected noise did not herald the approach of the enemy, or the springing of a trap. It was merely the striking mechanism going into action. The large paddle-wheel speed controller stirred a current of air as it spun round. One of the massive weights on the wall began to descend. The striking hammer clanged on a bell in the chamber above and the reverberations of the first stroke of the hour made Ian's ears sing.

The boys could not hear each other speak until the repeated clangs came to an end. Then, rather subdued by their experience, they crept down the spiral staircase. Ian locked the door and replaced the key in the pocket on the curtain.

'Are we going to tell Dad about this?' Roy asked as they walked to their bicycles.

'Not yet. He won't think we've enough proof for him to be able to arrest the Glovers. Let's go back to Beech Close and see if we can scout round the garage for those false number plates.'

Roy grumbled that it was his supper-time, but he was now sure that Ian really was on the track of the payroll gang, so he rode back to Beech Close with him. The matter of supper-time was forgotten.

The boys left their bicycles at the entry to the cul-de-sac and approached the Glovers' house on foot.   As they walked along Ian spoke in a low tone.

'I've been thinking about that clock business, Roy.   The Glovers went to a great deal of trouble to fix their alibi.   They needn't have gone to all that bother if other members of the gang had done the snatch, so I'm sure they did the job themselves.'

'But what about your Mini being found at Wimbledon?'

'That's a puzzle,' Ian confessed.   'Perhaps Mr Glover hid it close to Quarry Lane, nipped into town in his wife's car, with her, to establish his alibi, and then went back to Dad's car and drove it to Wimbledon.   Perhaps that's what Mr Glover was doing for the rest of the morning.'

Roy shook his head.   'Not likely, Ian.   The longer Mr Glover waited before scooting off the more he risked being caught on the road as the police alerted patrols.'

The front gardens of Beech Close were deserted now.   The claims of supper and television had drawn everyone indoors—even the Glovers, it seemed.   Their garage doors were closed, but the gates were open.

'Perhaps they've gone out,' Roy suggested.

'Or done a bunk.'   Ian turned in at the drive without hesitation.   'Come on, we'll try the back door.   If they're in we'll offer to wash the car again, but if they're out . . .'

He left the sentence unfinished.   Before knocking on the back door he looked through the garage window to check if the Mini was there.   It wasn't.

Ian at once tried the side door to the garage,

while Roy glanced apprehensively at the kitchen window.

' Do you think they're *both* out, Ian ? ' Roy was nervous.

' I expect so. Have you seen anyone moving indoors ? '

' No.'

' Then let's investigate.' Ian opened the side door but Roy hung back.

' We oughtn't to go into the garage, Ian.'

' I daresay not, but it isn't as if we're breaking in like burglars, or going into the house. This door is not locked and there are special circumstances.'

' All the same . . .'

' Oh, come on.' Ian was impatient, but he was also uneasy in his conscience. Roy was right. They ought not to poke and pry in the garage. But under the exceptional circumstances it was surely justified, and if the number plates could be found . . .

' Be quick, then. Just a glance round.' Roy closed the door behind him.

' Help me, Roy. Don't just stand there. We've got to work fast, before the Glovers come back— if they are coming back. You take the top of the bench, I'll root in these boxes underneath.'

From time to time as they searched Roy looked uneasily through the window into the little backyard.

' It's dark under the bench,' Ian complained. ' But I suppose we'd better not risk putting on the light.'

' Certainly not.' Roy shuddered at the idea.

The litter on the bench, and beneath it, was unaltered since Ian's last visit. The jam jars, the oily rags, the fir cones. All disappointingly the same. Ian glanced up, at the storage platform on the cross beams.

' That's the place, Roy, I bet. We must climb up there. Take the steps from beside the door.'

Roy looked at the folding steps, but shook his head. ' We can't open those, Ian. The Glovers may come back at any moment and find us here.'

' Well . . . perhaps we can manage to climb up from the bench.'

Ian clambered on to the bench and attempted to swing up to the roof platform, but it was too high.

' No good, Roy. We shall have to use the steps.'

' I don't like the idea.'

' Oh, come on. Don't mess about now, just when we're about to discover vital clues.'

Ian took the steps himself and opened them out. In no time at all he had nipped up them and was crouching on the roof platform, between the two trunks. He looked down at Roy, whose face was tense and pale with nervousness.

' Stand by the doors and listen, Roy. If you hear a Mini coming tip me off.'

' All right.'

Roy put his ear against the panel of the garage door as Ian began to ferret through the pile of oil paintings. They would make a good hiding-place for number plates, Ian thought, and seconds later his hunch was proved correct. Between a gilt-framed study of a bowl of roses and an oil painting of chrysanthemums he found two number plates.

At first he could only see them end on, but he gave a whoop of triumph as he dragged them out.

' I've found the plates, Roy. The evidence we need for your father. I shan't be a sec now.'

The number, he thought, would be that of the Glovers' Mini. But when he looked at the plates they bore the number of his father's car.

Puzzled, Ian squatted back on his heels. This was not the piece of jig-saw he had expected to find, but it surely fitted in somewhere. He fingered the strong spring clips, which had been used to hold the plates in position over the real number plates.

' Quick, Ian, they're coming ! '

Startled by Roy's cry of warning, Ian slapped the plates together and dropped them beside the pictures. He swung his feet down to the steps, but too late. The Mini was turning into the drive. A moment later it stopped just short of the garage doors.

' We're trapped,' Roy whispered.

' Come on up here. We must hide.'

' What about the steps ? '

' We'll pull them up after us. Hurry ! '

Roy didn't need urging. He moved swiftly. The key was turning in the lock of the garage doors as Ian and Roy completed the desperate task of hauling the steps up beside them on the platform.

The steps made the accommodation more

cramped and the boys were not able to stow them properly before the garage door opened and they had to freeze into silence, hardly daring to breathe.

Ian hoped the steps would not overbalance from their precarious angle, and that the oil paintings would not slither in a disastrous landslide. Both steps and paintings threatened to betray the young detectives at any moment.

Mr Glover opened the second of the large doors. His wife drove the Mini into the garage.

'I think I can hear the phone ringing, Doris,' Mr Glover called as she switched off the engine.

'All right, I'll get it.' Mrs Glover scrambled out of the car. 'Probably the Townswomen's Guild, about the play.'

Mrs Glover ran to the house. To Ian's annoyance her husband showed no sign of following her. With leisurely movements he opened the boot of the Mini and took out half a dozen beer bottles. Then he looked inside the car and produced two London evening newspapers. He opened one on the roof of the car and began to read. Ian, peering down with great caution, saw that Mr Glover was studying a report of the payroll snatch from Brown's van.

He continued to read until Mrs Glover came back.

'It was Mrs Cooper, Stan. She says Ian is late for his supper and she wondered if he had come here again to pester us, as he did last night.'

'Oh. What did you say?'

'I told her I hadn't seen him, but if he turns up I'll ring her back.'

' What do you mean, " if he turns up " ? You're not expecting him, are you ? '

' I wasn't, Stan, but Mrs Cooper's call reminded me of something.'

' Oh ? '

' You know those two bicycles that were leaning against a tree at the corner just now ? '

' I didn't notice them.'

' Well, I did, Stan. They were boys' bicycles. I told you Mrs Cooper said this morning while we were having coffee that her son suspects us of being bank robbers or car thieves.'

' The young blighter—do you think he's snooping round with his pal ? '

' I've a feeling something's wrong, Stan.'

' Now, Doris, don't panic. Everything's gone splendidly.'

Mr Glover sounded confident, but Ian noticed that he looked round the garage uneasily. So did Mrs Glover, and suddenly she caught her husband's arm.

' Stan, the steps have gone ! '

Ian became very conscious that the feet of the steps were projecting over the edge of the platform. But it was too late to move them now.

CHAPTER 10

ESCAPE

' ALL right, boys. I know where you are.' Mr
Glover sounded almost relieved. He jumped up
on the bench and peered over the edge of the
platform. ' What on earth are you doing up there,
eh ? '

Ian did not reply. There was nothing he could
think of to say, and it would not be much use
trying to bluff as the number plates were lying
beside the pile of old pictures. Mr Glover caught
sight of them. He hopped down from the bench
quickly.

' Stan—have they found anything ? ' Mrs Glover
asked anxiously.

' Enough,' Mr Glover answered grimly. ' Shut
the doors, Doris. Quickly.'

Mrs Glover ran to the large doors and closed
them, locking them from the inside.

' You know there isn't a key to the side door,
Stan. You can't shut the boys in here if that's
what you're thinking.'

' I've other plans, Doris. You nip in and phone
Mrs Cooper. Tell her Ian has turned up and
we're giving him supper so she's not to worry.
And tell her Roy's with him—ask her to pass the
news on to Roy's mother.'

' All right, Stan.'

Mrs Glover left the garage by the side door.

Her husband sat on the bench, on guard. He did not say anything, but took a large knife from his pocket, opened it, and felt the blade with his thumb menacingly. Ian and Roy exchanged uneasy glances.

'Been playing at detectives, have you?' Mr Glover snarled suddenly.

'Yes,' Ian answered.

'What made you suspect me?'

'I knew you stole our car, because I saw you in it yesterday at lunch-time. You passed me.'

'How do you know that was your car?'

'Because of the scratch on the door. I'd made the scratch with my bike on Saturday.'

'That scratch!' Mr Glover clicked his tongue. 'The one unforeseen thing. Pity you spotted it —I polished it out before I left home in the afternoon.'

He lapsed into a brooding silence and Ian took the opportunity of edging over to the trunk that was handiest, determined to find out more.

The lid was not fastened. Ian raised it and peeped inside. There was hardly enough light to see anything, but he made out the shiny domes of two crash helmets and some dark clothing.

'Stop poking about up there,' Mr Glover commanded irritably.

'I like poking about,' Ian retorted. 'There should be some more number plates up here—the ones you clipped on our car.'

Mr Glover laughed shortly. 'You won't find 'em.'

'What have you done with them?'

' Find out—if you're so clever.'

' The police will,' Roy snapped, annoyed by Mr Glover's tone. ' Your game's up.'

' Yes,' Ian said. ' We know you did the payroll snatch this morning.'

' You're wrong. I've got an alibi.'

' No you haven't,' Roy said. ' We've found out about the church clock.'

' Oh ? ' Mr Glover was taken aback.

' And there are some interesting things in this trunk,' Ian added.

' Leave those trunks alone,' Mr Glover snarled. He sprang to his feet and seemed about to attack the boys on the platform, but his wife came back at that moment.

' It's all right, Stan,' Mrs Glover reported. ' Mrs Cooper was pleased to hear the boys weren't making a nuisance of themselves. I said they would be here for an hour or so.'

' Good work, Doris. That'll give us plenty of time to get clear.'

' We've got to put Plan B into operation ? '

' Yes. A pity. If it hadn't been for these dratted boys we could have spent a quiet summer here unsuspected. Now we must blow—when we've taken care of them.'

' Stan, you're not going to do anything violent ? '

' Not if they're reasonable, but we've got to keep 'em quiet, Doris. Fetch the cases, and the clothes line from the kitchen cupboard. Better bring something for gags too.'

Mrs Glover hurried away. Her husband resumed his watch, glowering ominously, his broad shoulders and hefty arms a warning of his physical power if things came to a rough house. But Ian was determined to put up a fight and make a bid for escape.

Ian had other things on his mind too. Even in that critical moment he was a detective considering clues. The number plate and the clothing in the trunk seemed at first two pieces of the jig-saw that didn't fit, but suddenly he realised their full significance. Mr Glover had used his own Mini for the payroll snatch, with the number plates of Ian's father's car clipped on.

The stolen Mini had been parked at Wimbledon as a red herring, complete with duplicate skid-lids and clothing, to make the police think the gang had got away. And all the while the thieves were still in town, pretending to be innocent.

Ian lifted the lid of the trunk again. This time he glimpsed the goggles of two gas masks before Mr Glover bawled at him.

' Leave those trunks alone.'

' I've only looked in one yet.' Ian dropped the lid. ' Plenty of evidence there though. The clothes you used for the raid.'

' So what ? '

' So maybe the money is in the other trunk. Have a look, Roy.'

Roy eased over, moving the steps a little, and lifted the lid.

' It's empty,' he reported.

Mr Glover laughed. ' You don't suppose we'd leave the money out here, do you ? It's packed in our emergency cases, ready for us to take at a moment's notice. Just as well too, the way things have turned out.'

'You were hoping to live on here after the payroll snatch, as if nothing had happened ? ' Roy asked, astonished.

'That was the whole idea. I've seen too many crooks caught because they started running after a job. Once you start running you're vulnerable. I planned this job so that we could stay put until everything had blown over. Then we could have left without any hurry and gone where we liked.'

'Now you'll be on the run—and vulnerable,' Ian pointed out.

'We'll manage. I know how to disguise myself, and where to go. But it's a pity. Just spoils a perfect job.' Mr Glover shook his head sadly. 'A pity. Everything had worked out so well.'

'I still don't understand about the cars,' Roy complained.

'It's simple,' Ian said with a touch of impatience. 'Mr Glover used his own for the job, and ours for a decoy.'

'That's right.' A note of pride came into Mr Glover's voice. The vanity of a crook. 'I drove Ian's father's Mini to Wimbledon yesterday after- noon and parked it in a quiet spot, under false number plates. The clobber was in the boot— gas masks and skid-lids and so on. Then all I had to do this morning was to nip up to Wimbledon— the fast train stops there, you know—and drive the car round to park in the main road, after removing the false number plates and putting them in my brief case.'

' You caught the train from here soon after you'd been to the car park with your wife ? ' Ian queried.

' That's right. I disguised myself a bit—glasses and a cap and a moustache. I went to the station straight from the car park.'

' Your wife was the other "man" in the hold-up ? '

' Yes. She wore trousers and a dark jacket over her summer frock. When the snatch was over we drove a bit farther down Quarry Lane, whipped off our jackets and clobber, and the number plates of Ian's father's car, and then nipped into town and parked. We were in the park before the time of the snatch, as our ticket proved.'

' What about the false number plates on my Dad's Mini ? ' Ian asked.

' I dropped 'em in the Thames off Putney Bridge, on my way from Wimbledon.'

' I see.' Ian wondered if it would be helpful to push the nearest trunk over the edge of the platform, so that it fell on Mr Glover's clever head. ' But your alibi was thin, and you disappeared after you had been seen in the car park. I suppose your wife went to the clock, to see to the weights ? '

' Yes. She went to the church, then to coffee.'

' And then back to the church when it was time to replace the normal weight on the pendulum ? ' Roy asked.

' That's right. We worked out the exact times one night when we stayed up the church tower experimenting.'

' Weren't you afraid the police would suspect

you ? ' Ian queried. ' I mean, because of the mauve Mini, not the clock ? '

' They would naturally ask about our Mini, as they did. But we had an alibi, and were well known here, so they would rule us out. And with the stolen Mini found at Wimbledon, well . . . I figured the police wouldn't bother us again.'

' Are you the brains behind the big London gang ? ' Ian challenged.

Mr Glover looked pained. ' My dear boy, I don't belong to any *gang*. I work alone. What's the use of doing a payroll robbery if you have to split the proceeds with a large gang ? There isn't enough in it to make it worth while. No, I believe in organising a job with care and taking all the money myself. Everything would have worked perfectly on this job, if you boys hadn't poked your noses in. Still, all is not lost.'

' Not yet,' Ian said, edging the trunk along and catching Roy's eye.

Mrs Glover came back then, with the clothes line and one suitcase, which was evidently heavy.

' Ah, get the other case, Doris, then help me to tie up the boys. But just watch them while I stow this.' Mr Glover took the suitcase from her and put it into the car, on the back seat.

' *Now, Roy !* '

Ian pushed the trunk over. Mr Glover was half in and half out of the Mini. Mrs Glover was at the open side door of the garage. She screamed as the trunk fell.

It dropped between Mr Glover and the wall,

thrusting him farther into the Mini and wedging the car door behind him.

Roy might hang back when his conscience was uneasy or embarrassment threatened, but he was no slouch when it came to action. He pushed the steps over, and the oil paintings. They fell on the roof of the Mini with a most satisfactory clatter, drowning the roars of rage from Mr Glover. As a final bomb, for good measure, Roy added the empty trunk while Ian jumped down to the bench.

Mrs Glover had rushed to the help of her husband. Now she turned and tried to stop Ian in the doorway, but he pushed past her, followed by Roy.

' Quick, Roy ! The phone.' Ian dashed into the house, with Roy at his heels. They locked the back door behind them.

Then, while Roy put the catch up on the front door and kept watch, Ian phoned for the police. He spoke to Roy's father, who was for a few dreadful moments inclined to think Ian was pulling his leg. But Ian managed to convince him and the police went into action.

They arrived in two cars as the Glovers were backing down the drive after a desperate struggle with trunks, steps and pictures, to get the Mini out of the garage in a hurry.

The police found half the money from the pay-roll robbery in the suitcase in the Mini. The remainder of the money was in another suitcase in the house.

' A good thing I decided to take you seriously when you phoned, Ian.' Detective Sergeant

Kenton smiled. ' I very nearly didn't, remembering the coal-scuttle business.'

' I hope you'll forget that case now, sir,' Ian begged. ' I'm getting better, you see.'

' Sure it's not worse, my lad ? Well, run along. And don't ride too close to your father's car in future. If you scratch it again you'll be in dead trouble.'

Ian laughed happily. His pocket money and his holiday were now secure. So was his reputation as a detective.

Printed in Great Britain by
Thomas Nelson (Printers) Ltd, London and Edinburgh